JUN -- 2010

Ela A
275 Mc
(847) 438-3433
www.eapl.org

P9-DMU-307

31241008709456

For Mum and Dad and Isy

Thanks to Lee, Rachael, and Stephanie,
and everyone at Schwartz & Wade Books.

Copyright © 2016 by Ged Adamson

All rights reserved. Published in the United States by Schwartz & Wade Books,
an imprint of Random House Children's Books, a division of Penguin Random House LLC, New York.
Schwartz & Wade Books and the colophon are trademarks of Penguin Random House LLC.

Visit us on the Web! randomhousekids.com

Educators and librarians, for a variety of teaching tools, visit us at RHTeachersLibrarians.com

Library of Congress Cataloging-in-Publication Data

Adamson, Ged, author, illustrator.

Douglas, you need glasses! / Ged Adamson. —First edition.

pages cm

Summary: After visiting the eye doctor, a near-sighted dog gets glasses.

ISBN 978-0-553-52243-3 (hc) — ISBN 978-0-553-52244-0 (glb) — ISBN 978-0-553-52245-7 (ebook)

[1. Eyeglasses—Fiction. 2. Dogs—Fiction.] I. Title.

PZ7.A2315Do 2016

[E]—dc23

2015017776

The text of this book is set in Mrs. Ant.

The illustrations were rendered in pencil and watercolor.

Book design by Rachael Cole

Squirrel painting on easel on back endpaper by Rex Adamson

MANUFACTURED IN CHINA

2 4 6 8 10 9 7 5 3 1

First Edition

Random House Children's Books supports the First Amendment and celebrates the right to read.

DOUGLAS, YOU NEED GLASSES!

by Ged Adamson

schwartz & wade books • new york

Nancy and Douglas were chasing squirrels.

At least, Douglas *thought*
he was chasing squirrels.

You see, Douglas had always been a very nearsighted dog.

His bad eyesight often
got in the way of things.

He missed important signs.

Sometimes he even went
home to the wrong house.

But when a nice, innocent
game of fetch . . .

. . . ended in disaster,

Nancy said, "That's it, Douglas.
Come with me."

"Why are you taking me to
a shoe store?" asked Douglas.

"Douglas, this is the eye doctor,"
Nancy said. "He's going to help you."

"Now, Douglas," said the eye doctor.
"Tell me what you see."

"Dinosaur," said Douglas.

"Er . . . crab?"

"Flying saucer."

"Definitely a horse."

"Another dinosaur."

"That one's easy," said Douglas.
"A squirrel."

After the test, the eye doctor showed Douglas a cabinet full of glasses.

FASHION

NOVELTY

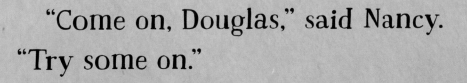

"Come on, Douglas," said Nancy. "Try some on."

At last, he found a pair that was just right.

Perfect!

On the way home, Douglas said,

"Wow! Everything looks amazing."

And it was.

REAL KIDS WHO WEAR GLASSES!

Want to show us how you look in your glasses? Ask an adult to help you post a photo on social media. If they use the hashtag #douglasyouneedglasses, we will definitely see it.